HEALING TRISTAN

TONYA CLARK

Copyright © 2021 by Tonya Clark

Publisher: Love & Devotion Author Services, Inc.

All rights reserved.

Print Edition ISBN# 978-1-949243-32-1

Healing Tristan is a work of fiction and does not in any way advocate irresponsible behavior. The book contains content that is not suitable for readers 17 and under. Please store your files where they cannot be accessed by minors.

Any resemblance to actual things, events, locales, or persons living or dead is entirely coincidental. Names, characters, places, brands, products, media, and incidents are either the product of the author's imagination or are used fictitiously. The author acknowledges the trademark status and ownership of any location names or products mentioned in this book. The author received no compensation for any mention of said trademark.

Cover Photographer: Tonya Clark Photography- All About the Covers

Cover Model: Travis Norwood

Cover Designer: Cover Lovin' Designs

Editor: Ink It Out Editing

CHAPTER ONE

Rickie

Five years ago, my world was turned upside down. I sat there looking around at all of the military brothers and sisters of my brother, as they stood at attention as we said our finally goodbye to a man who gave his life for his country. I just sat there, eyes dry; there were no more tears to cry as I watched them fold the flag that was draped across his casket and handed it to my sister-in-law, Becca. She was sobbing while tightly holding my niece, who then was only three months old. I could only close my eyes with each discharge of the rifles. I swear, my heart was beating with each one. There were no more tears left, I had cried every night since the day we found out my brother would be coming home. Looking down the line of soldiers, I noticed one who was in a wheelchair at the end of the line sitting as tall as he could. He was at attention with his follow soldiers. Next to him, was a soldier on crutches. It's when reality hits you how much these amazing women and men are willing to give up for our country!

I was in my fourth year of college, almost done with my degree for nursing. After the service that night, I went home and did a little research and that's what led me to my career today. Three more years of college, but I've been working with disabled soldiers now for a little over a year as a Physical Therapist. It's how I remember and honor my brother and what he gave up for his country. I wasn't the type to join the military and fight the battle my brother felt he needed to be a part of, but I can help those who have given a part of themselves to their country, and have the battle of recovery in front of them.

I was extremely fortunate to be offered the job I now work at and straight out of college. I was the top student in my class and was offered the opportunity to work at a rehabilitation center that was at the top of the list for advance treatment for wounded soldiers. I specialize in working with men and women who now live with a prosthetic limb.

Reading through the chart of my new patient, my eyes instantly go to the words, "Returning to Active Duty." With the technology today, it is completely possible for a soldier to return to active duty with a prosthetic limb; this will be the first that I work with though, and I have to admit, I'm a little excited. More so though, I'm very curious on why anyone would want to go back?

Captain Tristan Connell

Left Leg: Amputated below the knee

I read further into the Captain's file. Details on the injury and how sustained, the length of time since injured. There isn't much to go on, but at least it gives me a little information.

A text comes through on my phone, letting me know Captain Connell has arrived. I never get used to this part. Walking out to meet someone for the first time, my heart still jumps with nerves every time I meet a new patient. You never really know the extent of what the patient is dealing with by just a couple of words on a chart. Some are very open and sweet, others withdrawn and very hard to communicate with.

The strong voice echoing down the hall can't be missed. "Stop coddling, you don't have to stay."

"Sit down and wait, why are you so damn determined to push things? They want you in that chair for a reason, quit trying to hop around," I hear a feminine voice follow.

Sounds like a husband and wife squabble. Taking a deep breath, I round the corner with a smile on my face.

Walking into the waiting room, there are only two people there; the woman is standing and looking straight at me, the gentleman has his back to me when I enter. "Hello, I'm Rickie Eastman your physical therapist."

The man turns in the wheelchair and my breath catches instantly in my chest. Oh holy, wow. Dark hair, soft dark eyes, olive colored skin, and muscles pushing out of everywhere. His biceps, his thighs, his chest. Breathe Rickie, breathe. I find myself chanting in my head. Now you may want to blink. I lecture myself as I catch myself staring at the most beautiful man I think I've ever seen. His wife is standing right behind him and all I can do is stare at him.

"How long until I'm back with my team?"

I hear the voice, but can't really register the question in my head.

"Tristan, at least say hi first." The woman standing behind the chair reaches her hand out to me, "Hello, I'm Adrienne Connell."

His wife, Rickie enough, you are not being very professional at the moment. This clicks me out of my very unprofessional behavior. I'm finally able to blink and look up at the woman.

"It's nice to meet you, Mrs. Connell."

She laughs and shakes her head. "Sister, not wife." She gives me a knowing smile over her brother's head and I know I must be ten shades of red now.

I give myself a moment as I act like I'm looking back down at something in the chart that is in my hand. I need a moment to breathe and collect myself. "So, Captain Connell, it's nice to meet you."

"Tristan," he corrects me. "How long until I'm back with my team?"

I look up and see the half tilted smile on his face. He knows, but I didn't hide it well either. I basically stood there drooling over myself, so what am I expecting? Enough is enough, I'm a professional and I need to act like one.

Holding out my hand to him, he takes it and I have to keep my knees from buckling. What the hell is that all about? His smile widens as he watches me closely. He is seeing everything and I'm making a complete fool of myself.

Clearing my throat, I decide to try and flip this around a little. "Captain Connell, the time is all up to you and how hard you work."

"It's Tristan," once again he corrects me. "And as you will find out, I'm not afraid of a little hard work. Let's get started."

Pulling my hand out of his, I look back up at his sister. "You can either wait here, or come back in about an hour and a half. Today is more about fitting him with his new limb and paperwork, it will be an early session today, so hanging out might be better."

"Ms. Eastman..."

"You can call me Rickie," I try to capture the same tone he did with me, but it doesn't sound right, "Captain..."

"I'll call you Rickie when you call me Tristan," he interrupts me. "I need to get back to my team out on the field, what kind of time are we looking at?"

"Tristan," I emphasize his first name and I get that drop dead gorgeous smile as a reward. "You were just released from the hospital a week ago. I understand it's important for you to get back and I promise to help you achieve that, but we have a lot of work to do before you can return to active duty, so maybe we should work on patience first."

Adrienne laughs, "I like her."

"The sooner you can get me driving on my own, the better. So, she doesn't have to be around anymore." Tristan scowls at his sister and I can't help but laugh.

Without a warning though, my heart doubles in speed and I have to fight back the tears.

The bantering between a brother and a sister. Something I thought a person can never miss, is one of the things I miss the most. My heart slams against my chest and I have the need to turn and run out of the room, but these two probably already think very little of me as it is.

Keeping my eyes averted down as I try and keep the tears from falling I ask, "Do you need help getting down the hall, Tristan?"

I start to come around the back of the chair, but his voice stops me. "No, I'm fine, lead the way."

His voice is softer now and I'm surprised. I walk quickly in front of him, leading the way down the hall to our room where we fit the prosthetics.

By the time we get to the room, I think I have my emotions in check again. How many times can I embarrass myself in a matter of ten minutes?

CHAPTER TWO

Tristan

Something was wrong, I could sense it.

The moment I spun my chair around and placed eyes on Ms. Eastman, I knew I was going to be in trouble. Here stood this woman, sandy blonde hair and a bright, light color blue eyes. A color I had never quite seen before, but they were mesmerizing. Those eyes did all the speaking for her and if a person paid attention, you could read them in an instant. She liked what she saw and when she turned red from embarrassment, my hands itched to reach out and grab her, pull her down onto my lap, and find out how soft her lips were. Just as quick as I saw the lust in her eyes, I saw a sadness. She tried to hide it, but I caught the tears glistening in the corner of her eyes when she turned to head down the hall.

I could ask what was wrong, but that would be getting personal and something tells me that getting too personal with this woman would be a bad idea. Sure she is beautiful, but that would be a distraction. Right now, the one thing I needed to concentrate on is getting back to my team. So, when we entered the room and she turned, I decided to act as though I didn't see the moment of sadness in her eyes.

"Can you hop up on the table here?" Rickie points to the examining table. "I can get someone in here to help us get you up if you need some assistance."

I have a remark to that comment, but a smart ass remark and from the look that is still haunting her eyes, I decide now isn't the time.

"No, I got it."

Rolling my chair over to the bed, I push myself up onto the one leg I have now. It still feels very phantom to not be standing on two feet. I have the need to put my left foot down, as though it is still attached to my body, but I know if I tilt to the left, I'll fall to the ground. There is no longer a foot there to stand on. It's been this wheelchair and crutches for the past month and a half. I need to feel whole again. I know this prosthetic isn't my leg, but it will get me back on my feet and the sooner the better.

"So, with that thing I can walk again?" Rickie has what looks like a mechanical half leg in her hands.

"Yes, with the therapy and workouts you should be up and walking and with what I have learned just in a couple of minutes of meeting you, and your persistence to get back to your team, you will probably be running and climbing as well within the next couple of weeks."

"Couple of weeks?"

"Tristan, I know you want to be back on the field with your team, trust me I get it, but this isn't something we put on and you instantly are running around. You have a few months at the least of therapy, before you can even think about active duty again."

I want to scream, yell-- something. I hang my head to my chest and my hands grip the table tightly. It felt like everyone was making me hold back in the hospital and now it's going to be here as well.

Rickie's hand on my left knee makes me jump. I know the look in my eyes when they meet hers. I've seen it in the mirror a lot since I've been home. It is anger, fear, and pain.

"Sorry," she jumps back, "look, I promise you we will get you up and moving as quickly as possible. I'll push just as hard as you do, but we still need to make sure you are healed and ready. So, trust me when I say I'm on your side, alright."

My body relaxes and I feel the heat in my eyes cool. Something about this woman calms me. I nod and watch as she starts to approach with the bionic half leg in her hand. For a moment, I have disbelief that I will ever be back on the field. How am I supposed to do my job with half a leg missing? It's a fear I cannot allow anyone else to see. I've said from the moment I woke up, I was going to be back with my team, but at nights when I wake up sweating and wondering where I am, trying to take cover in my own bed, I wonder if I'm just lying to myself.

I had plenty of time in the hospital to do research about returning to active duty. With today's technology, it was giving soldiers a chance at as normal of a life as possible with missing a part of themselves, which now a days it included going back to active duty. My case being with only missing the lower half of one leg made my chances at returning the best.

"Alright, are you ready?"

She is standing in front of me with what looks like a large white sock waiting for me to make the next move.

I just nod, something about this whole experience has me nervous. Her fingers brush against the still healing and sensitive skin just below my knee and I jump. "Damn."

Ricky instantly jumps back once again. "Take your time, it's an adjustment."

"Quit telling me to take my time," my voice is loud and echoes through the room.

Ricky stands there just staring at me. She doesn't say a word. Surprisingly, her eyes aren't giving away to what she may be thinking.

The silence stretches for what seems like hours. She takes a more relaxed stance and just stands there in front of me waiting.

"Maybe I should find a different therapist?" I hear the irritation in my own voice and the anger.

Rickie's lips twitch up into a small and cocky smile. There is a fighter inside of there.

"Captain Connell," I start to correct her again, but she doesn't allow me to say a word, she just takes a step closer to me, leaving only inches between us. Those ice, white eyes staring straight into mine, that half cocky smile still formed on those amazingly full lips.

"You are the one who is holding this up, maybe now you will see that the only thing that will be holding you back from getting to your team, is you. Maybe now, you will understand what I have been trying to tell you. This has nothing to do with me, I'll work on your time. Now when you are ready, we will try it again."

My anger returns in full force, not at the spitfire that is in front of me telling me how it is, but at myself. She is right, and right now, she is daring me with her eyes for me to tell her otherwise.

"Should we call it a day and start again later?" There is an, "I told you so" tone to her voice.

I extend the remaining part of my leg past my knee toward her as my answer.

She nods with understanding and her eyes drop from mine and back to the task of putting the sock over my leg. The electrical shock when her skin touches mine is still there. I just do my best not to react to it this time it's the sensitive skin that is still healing I tell myself.

"This will help from rubbing on your skin. There will still be discomfort for a while, and probably a little pain, your leg is still healing. The more you wear it, the less discomfort you will feel."

I watch as she attaches the bottom half of my new leg into place. Then she steps back and watches me for a moment.

"How does it feel?"

"Surprisingly light." I swing my leg back and forth a couple of times.

"Does it feel too tight, or pinching anywhere?"

I just shake my head.

"Good, now you take it off and put it back on."

I look up at her with a questioning look.

"I'm not going home with you, but your new limb is, Tristan. I need to make sure you are good with attaching it to your leg."

She has me repeat the process at least a handful of times. "Alright, let's see if you can stand on it. Come down off the table on your right leg and hold onto my shoulders."

"You think if I'm going to fall, you would be able to stop me from hitting the floor."

"Captain, I'm a lot stronger than I look, now trust me."

Placing my hands on her shoulders, my eyes are locked with hers. She gives me a small smile and nods. Her eyes don't leave mine as I maneuver my body off the table and am now standing on my right leg, our bodies are in contact with one another. She seems even smaller now that she is so close. Her head is just above my shoulder and I have the need to wrap my arms around her and hold her tight against me.

"Alright, now I want you to slowly start putting your weight onto the left leg. I promise I've got you."

Her body being this close to me is throwing my senses in a whirlwind. I let go of her shoulders and grab the table behind me.

She doesn't fight me, she takes a small step back and watches, her arms stretched out in front of her like she is ready to catch a baby walking for the first time; that shot a punch to the ego a little.

I look down as I straighten my knee, the floor should

be under me now, but all I feel is the heavy and painful pressure on my knee and the remaining nub of my bottom leg. Something shifts and I feel my body pitch to the left. My knee buckles. I see Rickie reach out for me, but it's too late I'm falling. I feel her arms around my waist and we are both going down. She has twisted her body to take the force of the fall to the ground. Mere seconds is all we have and I know if I land on her, it's going to crush her. It's all happening in slow motion as I make one last effort on my right foot to twist my body around, as we fall, there is no way for me not to land on her, so I brace my arms out in front of me and pray that I can at least stop most of my weight from crushing her.

The bottom part of my body lands right on top of hers. I hear her swear quietly, but I manage to stop the rest of my body from crushing her with my hands on either side of her head in a push up fashion.

When I look down, her eyes are closed and her lips are pressed together. "Are you alright?"

She just nods her head. I'm not a small guy and half of me landed on her. "Rickie, open your eyes and talk to me."

That was my first mistake, because when she opened her eyes I felt a punch square in the chest. I knew I should move, make my way off of her, but her eyes looking straight up at me and her bottom lips sucked in between her teeth was doing something to me.

Before I could stop myself, I realized I wasn't pushing myself away from her, but closing the space in between us.

Her lips eagerly meet mine, that bottom lip popping

out from between her teeth. I'm pretty sure the groan that echoed through the room was from me.

CHAPTER THREE

Rickie

A year at this job and never once has any patient walked through the door and I wasn't able to concentrate on the only reason they were here. My job is to help our soldiers receive as normal as a life as possible after they gave up so much for our country. So, what in the hell am I doing on the floor, under Captain Connell, kissing him?

I get my hands up against his chest with every intent to push him away, but then his tongue finds mine and I find my hands aren't pushing him away, but grabbing onto his shirt as though he is a life line and I'm about to drown.

There is an object under his shirt that my hand wraps around, something sort of round and it hits me like a bucket of cold water-- dog tags. It's the reminder I needed. Becca gave me Jonah's dog tags and I remember holding them tight in my hands every night that I cried.

With a strength I didn't know I had, I push Tristan up and our kiss ends. I quickly work my way out from under him and up onto my feet. What in the hell was I thinking? How could I allow this to happen? Maybe he is right, I'll look into getting him a new therapist right away. He wants to get back to his team and active duty. I need to get him out of my head.

In one quick motion, Tristan pushes himself up with his arms and then is back to standing with his right leg, his left bent at the knee as he holds onto the exam table for support.

"Rickie, I'm..."

"I think we are done for the day. Please don't try and stand by yourself between now and your next appointment. I would suggest wearing the prosthetic during the day while in your chair."

"Rickie, let me..."

Again I interrupt, I don't think I want to hear an apology or an excuse. "I'll work on your request for a new therapist and you will receive a call with your next appointment date."

Tristan sits in his chair and moves toward me. I move to open the door, but surprisingly in that chair, he is quick. He stops me from opening it. "I don't want a new therapist."

"I think it's best." I can't look him in the eye. I've failed as a professional.

"Look, I'm sorry, Rickie. I don't know what

happened. It's been a whirlwind of a day. Please don't give up on me."

Vulnerability, something I wasn't expecting to see out of this beast and hard headed of a man. Again, he is tugging at something deep inside of me. Why is this so different with him? I've worked with good looking men before. Smart witted and funny, traits I would find very attractive and never have I had a problem with professionalism.

Now here I have a cocky, headstrong, and impatient man in front of me and I can't seem to keep my senses straight. "Don't give up on me." Those words slam me in the chest and I'm finding myself caving to him.

"Rickie, I promise it won't happen again."

Taking a deep breath, I know I'm making the wrong decision, but something is keeping me from making the right one. "Alright, let's go out to the desk. We will make your next appointment, but I think it's best if we call it for today."

When I open the door, he nods for me to go ahead of him. I can feel his eyes on me the whole way down the hallway and back into the waiting room where his sister is waiting.

"Wow, I'm glad I stayed, that wasn't long at all," she says, as she stands as we enter.

"Today was basically the fitting and some small directions, like I said earlier, this appointment is the easy one."

I hope she can't see through my intent to act like it was nothing big, but from the look she is bouncing between her brother and myself, I have a feeling I'm not hiding things very well right now. I make my way to the desk, make his next appointment for two days from now, and quickly leave as politely as I can. I need space from Captain Tristan Connell.

After work, I find myself at my sister in laws house with a pizza and a six pack of beer.

Becca answers the door. "Rough day at work I'm gathering from your text."

"Aunt Rickie," my name echoes through the house as Kinsley runs down the hall.

I have just enough time to hand the pizza off to Becca and drop the bag with the six pack onto the floor, before she launches herself into my arms with her little bear that she never lets out of her site.

My brother had a little bear in a military outfit made and a little message recorded inside when Kinsley was born. He said he wanted to make sure she knew his voice while he was away. He was deployed when she was born, was able to be home a week after she was born, but then had to go back.

I squeeze her tight and I hear the faint sound of my brother's voice from a bear that is squished between us, my heart ceases in my chest and I feel the tears threaten to escape. That is all the reminders I need, his voice and this amazing child tightly hugging me back. "How is my girl?"

"There is a boy at school who keeps taking my pictures that I color and not giving them back," she pouts.

"I think that means he likes you."

"Eww, that's gross, boys are gross."

See, now if only I could follow the thinking pattern of my five-year-old niece. Then just maybe, a hot military guy wouldn't be playing with my head.

"Kinsley, go wash up and get ready for dinner. Aunt Rickie brought your favorite."

Kinsley pumps her hand in the air and yells, "Pizza," as she turns away and runs back down the hallway.

"So, a six pack of beer, hard day at work?" Becca walks into the kitchen, grabbing a small stack of paper plates out of the pantry.

I really don't feel like getting into the details of the day's events. That brings up my brother and then the sadness in Becca's eyes, even though she always tells me you can't pick who you fall in love with. She has always said she has never regretted marrying my brother. He gave her the best gift anyone could, Kinsley. She is right and I understand what she is saying. We will forever have a part of my brother in that amazing little girl. She always tells me just because someone isn't in the military, isn't a certain binding contract that nothing will happen to them, and again, I know she is right. We have had this conversation so many times, I pretty much have her little speech memorized, but it's not just the possibility of losing them in the line of duty. I have seen firsthand what these men and women go through when they come back from combat, it's a long road to recovery, and sometimes that road can take some very nasty turns.

"Just exhausting I would say, couple new patients today, those are always some of the longer days." I choose to keep making out with a hot Captain out of the details.

CHAPTER FOUR

Tristan

"So, want to tell me what happened?"

Happened? Damn, I can still feel Rickie's lips on mine. What the hell was I thinking? I wasn't thinking, that was the problem.

"Silence, so I'm going to say that confirms my suspicion back there. You two entered that room like two teenagers that just got caught making out under the school bleachers."

"I think it's time I start driving myself, there is nothing wrong with my right leg."

"Yes, but you did just get out of the hospital from losing half of your left one, and that isn't saying anything about your internal injuries you had as well."

Adrienne and I have always been close. She doesn't sugarcoat anything and that is one thing I have appreciated since being home. She doesn't try and have the awkward conversation around my missing leg, she says it as it is.

"So again I ask, what happened?"

"We aren't having this conversation."

"I'm going to keep asking?"

She will too. "Fine, we kissed." I finally give in.

Her eyes go wide and her mouth drops open. "I knew it."

"Don't get excited, it was just a kiss, doesn't mean I'm going to marry her or anything."

"I can't believe you made a move on your therapist. On the first appointment."

"That makes two of us."

Looking over, I see the knowing smile she isn't trying very hard to hide. She directs her eyes for an instant down to my leg. "How does it feel?"

I look down at the new prosthetic that is now attached to my leg. "It feels foreign, that is the only word I can think of to describe it. It's not heavy at all, which I was expecting it to be. It will get me out of that chair and back with my team, so that's all that matters."

"Why are you so determined to get back? I get that you felt you needed to join, but don't you think you have given enough of yourself for your country? I mean literally," she points down at my leg.

"Don't start sis, you know how I feel. I get enough from mom. I don't need you starting on me as well."

The air in the cab of the truck gets thick and I think about bringing up what happened between Rickie and me to lighten it. My kiss with the doctor would be a lot less agonizing then talking about me returning to active duty. Adrienne hasn't said much about me returning. My parents haven't let the subject drop, but she has always just sat back and listened. I get that my family is scared, I was one of the lucky ones. I came home to heal, some aren't that lucky, but my team is out there and if there is anything the Army has taught me, it's to not give up on your family. My team is my family.

"Maybe you should look at things a little different, big brother. You have been given a second chance, you know better than most that there are men and women who don't get that chance. Maybe it's time for you to settle down, have a family."

I hear the pleading in her voice and it's tearing me up inside. I'm not mad at my family for voicing their opinions, or pleading, they might not believe it, but I understand what they are saying. Now, I just wish they understood where I was coming from and why I felt that I needed to return to finish out this tour with my team, but nothing I can say can give them that understanding. They received the phone call, they had to worry, and I know I am being selfish in wanting to return, but it's something I need to do.

Every night I wake up from the same dream. I don't remember the blast, or much before it. In my dream, I remember walking the area with my team, we have a couple bomb dogs with us sniffing the area, but I'm the one that finds one and I step right on it. I remember confirming the area as clear and had just turned around to head back to the vehicles. We were teasing one of our guys about his mom sending him a new pack of boxer briefs every time she sends him snacks. He is the new kid, and of course, an easy target. Then everything goes black. In my dream, that's what wakes me usually. The darkness. No sound. No pain. Just emptiness. The last couple of nights though, it's not the darkness that awakens me. Same dream, same darkness, same panic starts to set in. But instead, I'm settled by the softness of something against my body and lips.

Now, I'm standing here in between the parallel bars, two small hands on my waist, and that same soft body up against me supporting me as I take my first few steps on my new leg. My arms shake, but it's not from holding my weight up. I'm doing everything I can to not wrap them around her and claim those exact lips that I have been dreaming about the last couple of nights.

"You are doing great, Tristan," her reassuring voice brings my mind back to the task in front of me. Well, for a moment anyway.

She places her leg in between mine, her thigh rubbing up against mine, and the friction causes me to moan.

"Are you alright? Do you need to take a break?" Concern is laced in her voice.

I need a break from the direct contact of her body against mine, if I don't want to embarrass myself. I look down at her, there is genuine concern in her eyes.

"I'm good, maybe you should back up a little. I think I have this on my own."

She looks as though she is going to argue with me, but then she throws her hands up in surrender style and takes a step back. My body instantly misses the contact of hers and I have to keep myself from moaning again.

"Alright, a couple more steps."

She has been nothing but professional since I rolled in here today. She has made very little eye contact with me though, and that hasn't gone unnoticed. She has been polite, asking questions, and answering any I may ask, but that is where our conversation has ended. This shouldn't bug me as much as it is, but I want to shake her and make her look at me. Then I want to wrap my arms around that small waist of hers and pull her body back against mine again and remind her what we both felt the other day when we kissed. I wobble a little and her hands are instantly back around my waist.

"Rickie, I have this." My words come out between clenched teeth.

I hear the harshness in my own voice, but it's either back her away from me, or I embarrass the both of us right here in front of everyone in the center.

"Would you stop being so stubborn? I get it, you want to get back to the team, but you need to listen to me or you will end up on your back, Captain."

She only calls me Captain when she is trying to sound in charge. I don't miss her comment of me on my back either. I mean, she was the one on her back, but all the same I ended up with her lips as well.

CHAPTER FIVE

Rickie

I look up and see the smile in his eyes and that's when I realize what I just said. Instantly, my hands leave his hips and I take a couple of steps back. I've been trying very hard to be professional today. For the last couple of days, I've woken up out of dreams so steamy, I think I'm blushing in my sleep. Today having to work so close to him, his smell, his muscles flexing against my body as he takes each step, it has been very hard to be professional, when all I want to do is grab him by the front of the shirt and demand his lips on mine again.

"Fine, you think you got this, it's all you." I try to recover from my own slip up. As long as he thinks he has no effect on me, that's all that matters.

It's a challenge and one he isn't about to back down from. He takes the last couple of steps. I will admit, he is doing great. He is a little wobbly, but after I direct him to turn and walk back down the bars again to his chair, he has a pretty solid foot under him by the end.

"Good, go ahead and wheel yourself over to the machines, we'll get some muscle training in."

"I think I can walk there."

"Well, I'm asking you to wheel over there, let's not push it too much on the first day, Captain."

The challenging stare I'm receiving has me standing a little straighter myself. He wants to prove me wrong, that he can walk. I don't doubt that he can, but walking a couple of steps down the parallel bars doesn't mean he can go and run a marathon, or go back to his team already.

My heart constricts in my chest just thinking about him being back out there. I look down at the prosthetic leg and something lodges in my throat, fear! He has been out there, he walked right on top of a bomb that could very well have taken his life.

My brother's team was hit by a roadside bomb, it took the lives of four men and injured nine others. Listening to the stories of our patients when they come in has made a person see exactly how dangerous it is out there.

"I think you are holding me back. If I can walk, then why can't I walk? I'm getting a little tired of everyone telling me what I can and can't do. I'm the one who was blown up, I think I know if I can handle walking across the damn room."

"You pushing it too hard can actually set you back, Captain..."

"Damn it, Rickie, stop calling me Captain."

He's fighting me every step of the way today and both of our voices are starting to rise, we are catching the attention of everyone in the room.

Taking a step closer, I lower my voice. "You know what? I'm not going to fight you on everything. You won't listen to me, you are stubborn and honestly being an ass. I know how to do my job, Captain," I enunciate the word Captain, he wants to be stubborn, I can too, "If you want to get back to your team then you are going to have to start listening to me. Now, have a seat in that chair and head over to the machines."

One side of his lip tilts in a cocky grin, but he turns and goes to the wheel chair behind him. The feeling of satisfaction on my part is very short lived when he takes the brake off the chair and pushes away from him and it slams up against a wall that's close by. He turns to his left and starts to make his way to the weight machines.

I'm done! He doesn't want my help and I'm not going to be everyone's entertainment around us. If he thinks he can do this on his own, then he damn well can, I'm not playing this game.

One of the interns walks by. "Erin, can you please watch Mr. Connell for his remaining time here, then make sure he has his next appointment before he leaves with one of the other therapists."

She nods, but before she can say anything or ask any questions, I walk past her and out of the room. I need to get away from this man before I scream and really embarrass myself in front of everyone.

My office is the last one down the long corridor and it

seems a mile away. I have to keep myself from sprinting to my door.

Once to my office, I can't help but slam the door shut, oddly that helped a little. I stand in the middle and just take a couple of deep breaths. What is my problem? Tristan isn't the first impatient and stubborn soldier I've worked with or the rudest, so why he is affecting me like this?

My office door opens. Turning, I'm expecting the head of the program asking me what just happened, but it's Tristan. He shuts the door and turns the lock. My heart races and every nerve in my body comes alert. Why does this man have this kind of effect on me? I have no control of my own body when he is around. It hums for him.

We stand, a couple of feet apart from each other and just stare. The only sound is our breathing that fills the room. He sounds like he just ran a marathon, but he probably walked here just to prove his point, but what is my excuse?

"Tristan, please, just leave."

"Why did you leave me back there?"

"Because I'm not the one that can help you, you have made that very clear. You argue everything I say, you push me away, literally."

"Rickie, at the parallel bars, if I didn't get your body away from mine, I was going to take you right there and then without a care in the world to who was around to watch."

My eyes fly open in shock and I'm unable to move. He closes the distance between us, his arm wrapping around my waist, and pulling me up tight against his body. I put my hands on his chest with the intention to push him away, but his muscles flex under my hand and I find myself grasping onto the front of his shirt.

"Rickie, you have had this body pressed against mine in my dreams the last couple of nights, then I come here and it's like my dream becoming reality. You are pressed tight against me making concentrating on the task at hand very difficult, I needed you to step away."

"You walked in here." It wasn't a question, it was a statement, one that I needed to say to try and get my mind back to where it should be, and not on the man who I wanted to get lost in right now.

Our lips are brushing each other's as I talk. His lips brush mine as though he is testing my reaction, or waiting for me to make the next move.

CHAPTER SIX

Tristan

The last time we kissed, she pushed me away and I know she is fighting to do the same thing again now. I'm not going to be the one to make the first move this time. I lightly brush my lips against hers and her fist tightens around my shirt.

I have never chased after a woman before. If a woman wasn't interested, then that was just the way it was. Watching Rickie walk out of the room had me moving instantly. I can't let her walk away from me. I tighten my grasp on her waist and pull her in even tighter to me. She pulls on my shirt and claims my lips, her tongue instantly finding mine. She is now up on her toes, her pelvic thrusting into mine, her body language screaming at the barrier of clothing between us.

One minute she is trying to climb up my body, and the next she is pushing me away telling me to leave.

"Tristan, I can't do this."

I know she wants whatever is between us as much as I do, I just don't understand why she keeps pushing me away.

"Rickie, is it the whole doctor patient thing?"

"That should be it, but no, it's more personal than that."

Damn, the one thing I never even thought about is that she is in a relationship already.

"You are already with someone?"

She just shakes her head. I have to admit, I'm relieved. I'm not sure if I could walk away from her just because there may have been someone in her life already.

"Then what is holding you back? I know you are feeling the same as I am, I felt it in the way you kissed me, the way your body just begged for more. I felt it all Rickie, so you can't tell me there is no attraction, we both know there has been something there since the moment we met."

"You wouldn't understand."

"Try me!"

"There is no point. You are going back to active duty, I'm not one of those girls that does quick and fun, never have been. I get attached and then I get hurt."

Most men would probably use her words as the excuse they need to turn and run. I find her honesty refreshing.

"Rickie, no one is guaranteed tomorrow, I'm not looking for a one-time thing. I can't get you out of my head or my dreams. The last couple of nights when the darkness of the event closes in and there is no sound, no pain, just a black void, you press against me and remind me that there is life, that I'm alive."

"Are you listening to yourself, Tristan? Your dreams are dark and heavy and yet, you are eager to race right back into the situation leading to those dreams."

"You wouldn't understand, Rickie. No one does. I can't leave that family behind either."

"But you will leave this family behind. That makes no sense, Tristan. Your family has already gone through hell. They received that call. You give up and risk everything for your country. I understand, but once it has taken a piece of you, you decide to run in for more, why?"

"You wouldn't understand, you haven't been there."

"You are right; we haven't been there, but we have been in a fight with you guys."

Tears filled her eyes and my arms ache to reach out and draw her tight against my chest, protect her from anything that would bring that kind of sadness. But right now, I'm the one bringing tears to her eyes.

"What do you mean, *we?*"

"Families of soldiers, is the *we*, Tristan. We sit back here at home and wonder each time the phone rings or you hear a vehicle pull up in the driveway, if that's the news you dread the most. Every day I watch my niece grow up without her dad, my sister in law fight to keep it together, and raise a child without her husband. My parents hold on that much tighter to the only child they have left."

It's like a bulldozer just ran me over. Each one of her

tears that falls down her cheek is another punch in the gut. She lost her brother to this war.

My arms instantly wrapped around her shoulders and I pull her tight against my chest, hoping to absorb some of the sadness and tears. Her arms go around my waist and she buries her face into my chest. I'm not sure how long we stand like this, but I'll be her rock for right now, as long as she needs me.

Her sobs lighten and her breathing evens back out, she is calming down. She tries to pull out of my arms, but I just tightened mine around her tighter. I'm not ready to let her go. Her head comes up from my chest. Eyes brimmed red, cheeks wet from her tears, and pain from the loss of her brother in her eyes, breaks my chest open wide.

Something changes in her eyes, the sadness is still there, but something clouds it a little. Her eyes go from mine to my mouth and before I can wonder too long, her lips for the second time today claim mine, but this time it's slower, softer and this is the moment realization slams into me. This isn't going to be one of those quick and fun relationships either, I'm hooked.

CHAPTER SEVEN

Rickie

I didn't plan on telling Tristan about my brother, it just spilled out of my mouth and I couldn't stop the words. Being held against his chest felt safe and warm, and that's what I am going to say caused me to do exactly what I told him I didn't want to do. When I tried to pull away, he just held on tighter, when I looked up into his eyes, they mirrored the pain that mine held. I know he has lost friends during his time over there.

I couldn't stop myself from kissing him again, which was my first mistake. The second is when my hands made their way under his shirt and I was able to run them over his muscled abs and very well defined chest, that's when I lost the battle all together, now I needed him.

My hands trace some skin raised and my curiosity got the best of me. I pulled his shirt up and over his head, letting it fall where it will onto the floor. The raised skin are more wounds, some still healing. I lightly run my fingers over the multiple sections of his body that are marked as a reminder of what he went through. Leaning forward, I let my lips lightly kiss one of the angry marks still red. Tristan's hands are tangled in my hair and at the first touch of my lips on his skin, he pulls harder and his body tenses. I look up and instantly my lips are once again claimed by his, his tongue finding mine instantly. The room fills with the sound of our moans.

"Rickie, I can't stay away from you."

"Me neither."

"I need to feel you against me."

I raise my arms above my head as an invitation. My shirt is instantly pulled up and forgotten with his somewhere on the floor. Hands eagerly roam over my back, neck, and chest. His hand cups one breast while the other works on the clasp of my bra. My nipple hardens under the material begging for more skin to skin contact.

Once the barrier is removed, both of his hands fill with my breasts. His fingers lightly pinching each nipple, each hard and begging for more. Tristan's lips are everywhere, my lips, my neck, and finally what I was about to beg for, my breasts. His hair is short, nothing to dig your fingers into, so I press his head harder to me, begging for him to suck harder. His teeth tenderly bite down and I have to bite my lip to keep from making too much noise.

He has on running style shorts, so it doesn't take much to loop a finger inside his waist band on each side and slide them down his legs along with all remaining garments.

Scrub pants are in no way sexy, on anyone, but right now, I'm thankful for them. Stepping out of my shoes, Tristan is pushing down the remaining clothing that I have on. His hand traces a path back up my leg like a magnet to the heat, his fingers find what they searched for. I have to hold onto his shoulders to keep from falling to the floor as his fingers tease the fire that is already threatening to explode.

My hands begin to explore and instantly find the hardness pressed between the two of us. My thumb brushes over the tip and I feel the moisture already collecting there. Before I know it, I'm picked up and my legs are wrapped around Tristan's waist. Our lips find each other and as he takes a couple of steps, where to, I'm not sure or really care, but with each movement, our bodies rub together, his hardness against my heated core, and I'm not against begging for him.

He sits down on something, I'm not sure what. His thighs spread slightly, which opens me up more for him straddling him like I am. His arm lifts me slightly and when he brings my body back down to his, he guides himself deep into me, filling me completely.

Again, I bite down on my lip to keep from making too much noise. He pushes me back slightly, my hands now braced on his thighs, my breasts pushed out to him for the taking, his hands spanning my waist. His tongue circles one begging nipple. His eyes don't leave mine as he circles and teases one nipple and then gives the same attention to the other.

His hands slowly begin to move my hips. Then with a surprising force, he pulls my hips back to his, he is filling me deeper and deeper with each thrust. I sit up straighter, my fingers going to the back of his head, my nails biting into his scalp, begging him to suck harder.

I begin to take over the pace, lifting my hips just enough to fully take him back into me. His mouth leaves their quest and searches out my lips. His hands pull on my hips with each thrust, begging me to take him in more and more with each motion.

I can feel myself tightening around him. He takes my bottom lip between his teeth, his one hand comes back to the nipple of one breast. I lift my hips one last time and as I take him in as deep as I can, he bites my lip and pinches my nipple, the sensation together sending me into a spiral I have never experienced. His arm tightens around me and I feel each pulse of my explosion, pulling him deeper and deeper inside. He groans against my mouth and he finds his release with me. My legs are wrapped tight around him, his arms vice-like around me. Our foreheads are pushed together and the only sound in the room is our breathing, which is the silence that gives me a moment to pause and realize what we just did.

What the hell did I just allow to happen? He is still deep inside of me and our breathing is labored and I'm starting to panic. What makes things even worse, is that I'm in my office at work, with my patient! I need to pull away, but my body is screaming at me to not even think about it. How can this feel so right and so wrong at the same time?

I was emotional. He was here, things got out of control, and I am the one who instigated this. I made the first move. I kissed him first, I tore his shirt off, I can't be mad at him for anything. I allowed this all to happen. Actually, I begged for this to happen.

"Rickie, are you alright?" his voice is husky, and his concern makes me want to cry.

Am I alright? No! I am freaking out, I just broke every rule I've put together when it comes to men. The most important rule broken; don't get involved with a soldier and here I am wrapped around one, literally!

His arms loosen around me and he tries to pull back enough to look at me, but I keep my head buried into his chest. I can't allow him to see the shame in my eyes because none of it is directed at him, this is all me.

"Rickie, you need to talk to me."

I need to get myself together. I try to move my hips back on his legs, but his hands on my hips keep me right where I am.

"Tristan, please let go of me."

"Not until you talk to me."

"There is nothing to talk about, this should never have happened." I push away from him and almost fall to the ground as my feet look for the ground.

I quickly find my clothes. Keeping my head down, I get dressed. "Will you please get dressed before someone walks in?"

Out of the corner of my eye, I see him stand up from my desk and pull his shorts back up. The embarrassment burns my cheeks as I realize he didn't even remove his clothing, they were around his ankle this whole time.

His shirt is next to mine on the floor. Grabbing it, I hand it to him. "Are you going to keep ignoring me?"

"I'm not ignoring you, I'm trying to get dressed before

someone walks through the door and I get fired." I'm surprised I don't rip the seams to my shirt as I shove my arms through.

Tristan grabs my arms and pulls me back to his chest. My body instantly reacts with a need for him again. This is insane, my own body is fighting me on this.

"Rickie, stop and look at me."

Taking a deep breath, I try to calm my racing heart, at least now we are both dressed. It doesn't look as obvious that I just attacked this man in my office. Although, I'm sure it's written all over my face if someone were to come in.

Finding the courage to finally look this man in the face I ask, "What?"

"No, don't do that. Don't look at me like this was no big deal."

I needed him to leave before I lost it. I'm fighting the tears as it is. "I need you to leave, please."

"Don't send me away without us talking, please."

"Tristan, I need you to leave, there is nothing to talk about."

"The hell there isn't. We just had sex, Rickie."

I flinched as though I had just been slapped in the face.

"Yes we did, Tristan. We had sex, against everything I was standing strong against and I broke every one of my own rules. You are leaving and going back to your team, we both need to forget this ever happened."

"I don't think it's going to be that easy."

He was right; something about this man tugged at my heart. From the moment I walked in and saw him, something happened inside of me. Sure, he was good looking, but something else was there and I have felt it from that first moment. Now, after this I need to back away and quick, or I'm going to end up falling extremely hard for this man. And I can't, because he is leaving.

"If you aren't leaving, then I am."

Before he can stop me, I go to pull the door open and remember he locked it. At least no one would have been able to just walk right in. Turning the lock, I throw open my office door flinching as it slams against the wall. I don't look back, I make my way down the long hallway, and right into the therapy room. Lots of people are there, even if he followed me, there would be too many people around.

It's not right and it's what I wanted, but after fifteen minutes of waiting for Tristan to walk in, I realize he didn't follow me. Relief and hurt are a powerful combination of feelings to have at once. It's for the best, I know that, but it hurts. Why did it have to be him? Why the man that has to continue the battle? My heart wouldn't be able to handle it.

CHAPTER EIGHT

Tristan

How I ended up at the old drive-in, I'm not sure. I don't even remember leaving the parking lot of the therapy facilities. I'm not sure of how long I've been sitting here. I do know one woman has walked into my life and made me question every decision I had my mind set on in just the couple of days that I have known her.

From the moment the doctors told me there was a possibility of me returning to active duty, I knew without a doubt that was what I wanted. To finish out this tour with my team. I've heard my parent's arguments. I didn't think they understood, but after today, I realize I might need to think about things a little more.

Rickie had lost her brother to this fight. He didn't get to come home just missing part of his leg and a few new scars. He gave the biggest sacrifice; himself. When she looked up at me with the pain in her eyes, I lost my balance and had to find solid ground. One foot and a piece of metal. That was all that was holding me up.

I haven't spoken to anyone about that day, I don't really remember it. I do remember waking up in the hospital. Feeling the empty void of the bottom half of my left leg, every muscle in my body reminded me of what had happened from pain that shot through my entire body. The first question I asked the doctor was, if I could rejoin my team. I now remember hearing my mother's cry and my dad's curse, but I ignored it, and had a one track mind on what I wanted, to finish my tour.

It's dark out, and while I have sat here I have realized one thing. I understand more of what they are feeling and I need to sit down and let them know that. But I need to have my family understand why I need to finish this out. I can't live in fear just because of what happened, that is letting the other side win. I need to finish what I have started and pray they understand.

There is Rickie. I know she wants me to walk away from this, act like it didn't happen, but that isn't going to happen. I need her to understand as well. I understand her fears of me going back and I know it's not fair to ask her to wait for me to come back with a promise that I will be done after my tour is done. I will only have a couple months remaining once I return. I want her to be a part of my healing before I go back and after today, I realize I'm not just referring to the physical part of my healing. I want to be a part of her healing as well. No one can replace her brother, but someone needs to be there when she needs a chest to cry into on those days the memories hurt and I want to be that person. I just need her to understand what I need to do to heal as well.

It's been a week and I haven't seen Rickie at any of my appointments. I was told she had to take emergency time off and that I was scheduled with a new doctor. I almost laughed when I walked in and was greeted by an older gentleman. She made sure I was appointed to a male this time, no chance of kissing him during our sessions.

I thought about waiting it out until she returned, but I wanted to get the healing rolling. The sooner I could get back with my team, the sooner I would be home. It was on the second week I started to get impatient with everyone inside of the facility. No one would tell me anything about Rickie. She couldn't hide from me forever and I doubt she would be wasting this much sick time over us having sex. That's when I caught a glimpse of her. She was back to work, not sure how long she had been back, and I happened to look up just in time to see her walk past the windows that show out into the hallway, she was heading back to her office. I used the lame excuse that I had to use the restroom and stepped out of my session for a moment. At her office door, I tried the handle, it was locked. I knocked and listened, but nothing.

"Rickie, this is crazy, I saw you today. We need to talk."

Not a sound came from inside. Maybe she went somewhere else, but I wasn't leaving until we talked today. Finishing my workout and figuring she wasn't going to leave until the facility closed anyway, I grabbed a quick shower, changed, and headed outside to wait. This hiding game she is playing is ending today, we were going to talk.

CHAPTER NINE

Rickie

He saw me. I know he did and it didn't surprise me when he knocked on my door only a couple of minutes later. I took a couple of days off. I needed to get my head cleared up. I had watched his scheduled appointments and made sure I wasn't in the therapy gym when he was. I needed to separate us and this was the only way I could do it. I couldn't trust my own body to be around him.

The day was over and I was ready to be home. Walking out the front door, I was greeted with a sight that took my breath away. Standing on the wall overlooking the walkway looking amazing, is Travis. He has on dark jeans and a red shirt that shows off his arms. His sunglasses are covering his eyes.

"You know, the first day I met you I saw this woman who wasn't afraid to speak her mind. She didn't allow a wounded warrior with a little too much ego to chase her away, she raised her chin and took on any challenge he dished out with a fire in her eyes that I couldn't look away from. Didn't really take you as someone who hid."

"I'm not hiding." Yes I am. Who do I think I'm fooling? Definitely not Tristan.

"Really, then why haven't I seen you in the last couple of weeks? They said you had an emergency. Is everything alright?"

His concern pierced my heart, this is why I needed to stay away. He wasn't making it easy to not fall for him harder than I already am.

"I'm not going to lie to you, Tristan. I needed a little time to think."

A couple of staff members exited and I realized how out in the open we are at this moment. This isn't something I really wanted to talk about with an audience. I couldn't hide any longer, we needed to talk.

Looking over at the gazebo, we have on the side of the building, it looked like a good place to talk. No one was there, it was out in the open, so maybe just maybe I can control myself with this man.

"We can talk over there." I nodded my head in the direction of the gazebo. "A little more private than standing here in the front entrance of the building."

He doesn't say a word, just turns and starts walking, that's when I notice how well he is walking now. For someone who doesn't know him or what he has been through, they wouldn't even know that he is walking with a half bionic leg. It proves his determination to get back out on the field and with his team.

Leaning up against the railing, he waits for me to join him. "Ready to talk," he asks?

I take a seat in one of the chairs, keeping distance between us. "I know and I'm sorry. I needed a little time to think, plus hide from my embarrassment."

"Embarrassment, why?"

"Tristan, I not only basically attacked you in my office, but we had sex. I had sex with my patient. I broke so many company and personal rules."

"Do you regret it?"

"Only for one reason."

There will be no more lying to him or hiding. I need to let him know where I stand.

"What's that one reason, Rickie?"

"I'm having a really hard time staying away."

His brows draw in and he stares at me for a moment, like he is trying to decide if my reason is a good thing or bad. He pushes off the rail and starts to close in the space between us. Quickly standing up, I move to behind the chair keeping it between us.

Putting my hands up to stop him I say, "Tristan don't, please."

Stopping he looks at me confused. "Why do you need to stay away? Rickie, I don't want to stay away, there is something between us."

He feels it, but how couldn't he? Whatever is pulling us together has been there since the moment I walked into the room and met him for the first time. I may have been the one to make the first move and kissed him, but he kissed me back. The sex, oh my good gosh, the sex.

Two people don't connect like that unless there is more there.

"Tristan, you are going back." My voice cracks and my chest suddenly hurts. I'm already attached, even with the distance between us, I know what's going to happen if I ever find out something happens to him.

"Rickie, it will only be for a couple of months. I'm just finishing this tour. I know you don't understand, but I have to finish this out."

"You are right, I don't understand, but that isn't what matters. I would never ask nor expect you to stay just because we had sex. You believe you need to go back then you need to go. You need to understand that I can't allow anything between us build."

"Rickie, we like each other that's obvious."

"I'm not denying that, Tristan. I know we don't really know each other real well, but I can assure you I don't make it a habit of having sex with a men I don't know, especially at work and in my office."

"There hasn't been even a second that I thought that. I'm not that way either. I don't bounce from woman to woman."

Relief washes over me, but hearing him say it had me feeling conflicting emotions. At least if he was a player, it may make this a little easier to walk away from.

"I can't do this, Tristan. I'm not going to say or even assume I understand your reasons for needing to go back after what you went through. I respect you decision to return, but because of that, whatever may have started between us needs to end."

"You can't wait?"

"It's not about waiting for you to come home. It's more about waiting to see if you come home."

"Rickie, you can't..."

I stop him before he tells me I can't compare what happened to my brother to what may or may not happen to him.

"I see what my sister in law is going through. She is so strong for my niece, but I'm not sure if I can be as strong and there is no child involved. I'm not going to hide things from you. I can't shake these feelings you make me feel and it scares the hell out of me. I can't feel that kind of loss again, Tristan."

I can't stop the tears, they have burned the back of my eyes for too long and I let them go. Tristan is around the chair and pulling me into his chest before I can stop him. His arms wrap tight around me and he holds me as my tears soak the front of his shirt.

Tears of pain, sadness, and loss. If it hurts this much now, then I am definitely needing to read the signs and let him go.

"Why did you need to be brought into my life now?" my voice is muffled against his chest.

"It was time for us to find each other."

It's not fair, this is a cruel joke. Pushing out of his arms is not the easiest thing to do. I feel safe in his arms, it feels right, but I need to push away now before I can't.

"Rickie, nothing is going to happen to me."

"You can't guarantee that. You cannot make any promises, because that isn't a fair fight out there and no one knows what will happen."

"Rickie, that is life in general."

I know nothing in life is guaranteed, I'm not naïve. "Tristan, I'm not going to stand here and beg you not to go back. It's something you need to do and you should be the only one to make that choice. I think I may very well be falling in love with you and because of those feelings, I do need to ask you to tell me goodbye."

CHAPTER TEN

Tristan

In the last couple of months, I have endured a pain that I was pretty sure nothing could compare to. I was wrong. Rickie just tore my chest in two and it about dropped me to my knees. Her eyes are begging me to let her walk away. She just told me she is falling in love with me and follows it up with telling me I have to let her go.

"Rickie, please believe me when I say that I understand your fear. Can I stand here and tell you that there isn't a fear in me about going back. It's one of the most terrifying things I will do, but I need to face it. I can't let them win."

"I'm not going to tell you not to go, I have said that. I understand you have reasons and I will support you by not asking you to choose. I never want you to resent me, but you need to understand my feelings as well, Tristan.

You have your reasons to go and I have mine to walk away."

Can I let her walk away though? Could my feelings for her be enough that if I decide to stay I wouldn't regret that decision?

"Don't...," she cuts into my thoughts.

"Don't what?"

"I see your mind working, Tristan. You are asking yourself if you would have regrets. The need to ask yourself that is your answer. At some point, you would regret your decision and I'm not going to be that reason and have you resent me for it. It may take a little while to happen, but it would."

"So, you are telling me you won't have any regrets to walking away?"

Her eyes glass over one more time as she fights the tears and I know my answer, this is tearing her up inside and I see that shining through her eyes. Surprisingly, her lips claim mine. Her fingers dig into my hair at the back of my head. I feel the wetness from her tears roll down between our cheeks. The moan that echoes between us is etched with pain and it cuts into my chest.

"You need to go back," she whispers against my lips.

"I'm coming home, Rickie."

"Tell me goodbye."

"I can't."

She pushes up onto her toes and whispers in my ear, "Be safe."

She kisses my cheek and then quickly pushes away from me, running in the direction of the parking lot. I want to go after her, shake her until she agrees to wait for me, but that is being selfish. She is understanding my need to return to duty and I need to understand her reasons to walk away.

I'm not sure how long I've been sitting in the driveway, but my sister's worried look when she hops into the passenger seat tells me it has been a little while.

"Mom is concerned."

"I'm just thinking."

"Want to talk about it?"

Shrugging, I continue to stare out the front window of the truck at nothing. If I tell my sister what happened between Rickie and me, she will use it to fight the battle of keeping me home. I can't expect any of them to understand, but I would be lying if I said I haven't been second guessing my choice as well.

"You love her don't you?"

Another thing I have been asking myself while sitting here. I've never really been in love before. Few girlfriends in high school, nothing serious. I enlisted as soon as I graduated. I busied myself with moving up the ranks of the army.

"Why do you think that?"

"Tristan, you are second guessing your choices right now, it's written all over your face. You have been arguing with Mom and Dad since you woke up in the hospital about going back to active duty. There hasn't been a moment you hesitated when stating your points in those arguments. Here you sit in a battle with yourself, it can only mean one thing. You have fallen in love with her."

"I need to finish this tour, Adrienne."

"Did she ask you to stay?"

Shaking my head, I answer her question.

"Ok and what she won't wait for you to return, it's only a couple of months?"

"Her brother died a few years back serving. He left behind a wife and child. She says she can't do that."

"Then I think you need to let it go."

"I'm not sure if I can."

"Did you tell her how you feel?"

Again, I only shake my head to answer her question.

"So, what are you going to do?"

"I know none of you understand my need to return, but it's something I need to do."

"I've stopped that battle with you. I may not like it or understand, but I know you and if you don't go then you will regret it."

"That's what Rickie said."

"She loves you."

Rickie's voice echoes through my head as she tells me she is falling in love with me. "Look, don't say anything to Mom or Dad, this will just give them fuel for their argument against me going."

CHAPTER ELEVEN

Rickie

It's been a month since the day I walked away from Tristan. Every time I walk out of the center, I see him standing up on the wall leaning over the rail. It's an image that will be burned into my mind forever. My heart jumps every time I walk in or out of that door. He finished his therapy about two weeks ago and I haven't seen or heard from him since.

I couldn't keep scheduling patients around his schedule, so there were a few days I would be working with someone and feel his eyes on me. I have driven home in tears more times in the last month then I can keep count of. I'm not sure why I thought this would be easier. I had asked his therapist if he had been released to go back, and he confirmed he had passed everything and would be returning to active duty.

I have been homesick with the flu for the past two days and all it has done is give me more time to sit in my empty house and think about Tristan, wondering if he is alright. If anything was to happen to him, I would probably never know.

I was even tempted once to look over his file for an emergency contact number to call, but what would I say? Hi, I fell in love with Tristan and want to know how he is doing. Plus, I walked away, so I wouldn't know, I'm regretting that decision now.

My doorbell echoed throughout my house. I contemplate just letting whoever it is to think I'm not home and just go away. I'm starting to feel a little better, but yesterday I did the same thing. It was back full force early this morning. I hate being sick.

Again, the doorbell echoes. "Alright, I'm coming, give a sick woman a chance."

Opening it, I find Becca and Kinsley, "Oh honey stay out, I don't want either of you to get sick."

Holding out a bag to me she says,, "Mom said you weren't feeling well. I thought I would drop off some crackers, soup, and 7-up. How are you feeling today?"

Taking the bag she has handed me I look inside. "I'm getting better I think."

A box at the bottom of the bag catches my attention, but before I can pull it out, both my sister-in -law and niece walked past me.

"Becca, I don't want you guys sick."

"How are you feeling?"

Damn she is stubborn. "Right now I'm feeling alright, tired is all. I woke up around two this morning and have been leaning over the toilet until about an hour ago. Same thing yesterday. This flu is terrible, I don't want to sound ungrateful because I love you for the care package, but I really don't want either of you to get this."

Becca proceeds to walk over to my couch and sit down, pulling Kinsley up onto her lap, her little bear tight between the folds of her arms. My eyes instantly well up with tears. Now I'm thinking about my brother and Tristan.

"Aunt Rickie, you want to hold my teddy, he will make you feel better." Kinsley holds her bear out to me.

The tears stream down my face. What the hell is wrong with me?

"I'm pretty sure you aren't contagious."

I'm not sure what Becca means. I've been throwing up for two days. I thought yesterday it may have been something I ate, but when it returned this morning, I was pretty sure it was the flu.

"How late are you, Rickie?"

Late, for what? Why is she looking at me with that knowing smile? I think I need to take a nap.

"Late for work you mean? I'm not going in today."

Becca is shaking her head, "I'm not talking about work, Rickie, how late are you?"

I reach into the bag and start pulling the crackers and soup cans out, next the six pack of 7-Up. My hand brushes against the box I saw earlier. Pulling it out, my heart falls to my feet when I realize what she bought. Becca's words echo through my head, "How late are you?"

I think back and try to remember when I had my last

period. Holy crap! My hands begin to shake and I'm pretty sure if I don't find a way to take a breath, I'm going to pass out.

"That's what I thought. Rickie, breathe, nothing is for sure yet." Becca tries to calm me down, but it's not working.

"Mommy, what's wrong?" Kinsley squeezes her bear and my brother's voice fills the room.

Dropping everything, I make a fast dash to my room. This can't be happening. I can't catch my breath and the room is starting to spin. Plopping down onto my bed, I look around like I'm going to find the answer somewhere, but what answer I'm not sure.

Becca comes in and sits next to me. "Rickie, you need to calm down and breathe before you pass out and I have to call 911, let's not scare Kinsley with that, please."

"We only had sex once, Becca."

She laughs a little. "Rickie, how many times do you think it takes?"

"This cannot be happening, I can't be pregnant."

Becca holds up the box with the pregnancy test on the front of it. "There is only one way to find out for sure."

"I'm not as strong as you, Becca, I can't raise a child by myself."

"Alright stop! Rickie, who says you will raise the baby by yourself. I know I don't know this guy Tristan, but I'm sure he isn't going to walk away."

"He is back to active duty, Becca, what if he doesn't make it home?"

"Rickie, you can't live in this fear because we lost

Jonah. There isn't a day that I regret marrying your brother and having that amazing little girl out there. Do I miss him? Every minute of every day, but I wouldn't change anything. I would have still married him. You can't live life in fear of the "what if's", you need to live for all of the amazing times you will have. No one knows how much time they have."

"I don't know if I can live through that pain again."

"Rickie, I get it; you are scared, but you are a strong woman. Kinsley has been my saving grace since we lost your brother. I have a piece of him with me all of the time and I'm so very thankful for that precious gift your brother gave me."

"He is gone, Becca. I have no way to reach him."

She holds the box up to me. "Let's do step one first, we will worry about the following steps after that."

"Aunt Rickie, are you O.K.?" Kinsley's little voice fills the room, as she runs up to my bedroom door.

Wiping the tears away I smile at her. "Yes honey, Aunt Rickie just needs to pee."

Five of the longest minutes of my life pass as I stand there and stare at a little white stick. I didn't need the five minutes. That little pink plus sign pretty much popped up as I was peeing on the stick. I just thought if I gave it five minutes, it may disappear, nope. I believe it just became brighter.

Walking out, Becca knew without me having to say a word. Walking over she wraps her arms around my shoulders and hugs me tightly.

"It's going to be alright."

. . .

It's been a week and I'm still not sure if I believe it. I'm pregnant and with Tristan's child. A man I fell in love with in less than two weeks, never got a phone number, never met his parents. I did, however, meet his sister, briefly. We had amazing sex in my office, I told him to then go fight the war he needed to be a part of, and haven't spoken to him since. However, now I have this little person growing inside of me that is a very large part of him.

I have been staring down at the piece of paper from his file that has both of his parent's and surprisingly sister's contact information on. We usually only need one emergency contact, but Tristan decided to be very thorough and leave all three. I have no excuse to why I haven't tried to get a hold of Tristan.

I wonder if I should just wait until he gets home. He is back to active duty there is nothing he can do about it now anyway, he has to finish his time out there.

Becca and I have had many arguments about this. My mom and dad want to know how I got pregnant by a guy they have never met. My dad wants him back just to have the father to man talk. I can't even say boyfriend.

My mom and I did sit down one day last week and have a long talk. She understands where I am coming from, but like Becca, she says I can't live my life in this kind of fear. I just want to know why it had to be a soldier and one who is the most stubborn and determined you can find. Survives serving his country only to ask to go for round two.

I know the answer though. I fell in love with a man that

loves fully. He didn't want to leave his team, or as he called them family, behind. He wanted to finish what he started. He didn't want to live in fear of what it might take from him. His strength and drive, his honor, is what I fell in love with, even his sarcasm and hotheaded ways are all reasons I fell in love with the soldier who wheeled himself into my life a couple of months ago, and then foolishly allowed him to walk out of my life because of my fear of losing him.

Looking up at the clock, it was time to go home. Grabbing the paper off my desk, I place it in my drawer for tomorrow. Maybe that will be when I get enough nerve up to make the call.

Waving goodbye to the receptionist, I make my way out the door. Again, like every day the image in my head of Tristan standing there instantly pops up. Once again, I fight the tears that burn the back of my eyes. Pregnancy makes a person damn emotional. It's going to be a long nine months.

"Am I still getting the silent treatment?"

The voice wraps around me like a warm blanket. Damn, now I'm not only seeing him up there every day, I'm hearing his voice as well.

"Rickie, we need to talk."

That's not my imagination. Stopping, I turn and it's like deja vu, standing there leaning over the rail in dark jeans and a red t-shirt that hugs all of his muscles, is the man I fell in love with. The tears can't be held in, they stream down my cheeks.

Tristan quickly makes his way under the bar and hops down to where I'm standing. Wrapping me up tightly against his chest. I can't stop the tears. He is here and holding me.

We stand in the middle of the walkway like this, for I'm not sure how long. I have no care in the world to how many of my coworkers have walked by us.

"Hey, come on look at me." His voice is a whisper.

It takes a couple more seconds, but I manage to get the tears under control. Looking up, I claim his lips. No words can be said for what I'm feeling right now.

I feel my feet leave the ground, he has picked me up and is walking, and my lips don't leave his.

CHAPTER TWELVE

Tristan

I wasn't going to stand in the middle of the walkway while people made their way around us. Picking her up, I walk us over to the gazebo, seemed fitting actually.

I wasn't expecting this reaction from her when I decided to come here today. It's been a month and I was expecting and ready for anything, except her kissing me.

Setting her down, our lips part and she buries her face into my chest.

"You know one of these days, I'm going to be the one who makes the first move."

Her shoulders shake, I think she is laughing, but her face is still buried in my chest, her hands have a very tight grip on the front of my shirt.

"I can't believe you are here," her words are muffled.

"Hey, look at me."

It takes a second, but finally her head comes up. "I thought you had gone back to your team."

"I was on my way, actually. Sitting on the plane even, but something stopped me."

She looks up at me puzzled. I understood, it sounded crazy to me as well.

"I was sitting there, the plane was ready to take off. They were getting ready to shut the back ramp and it was like someone grabbed my arm and pulled me off the plane."

"What?"

"Trust me, I have had the same question. Last week was one hell of a week."

"What day were you leaving?"

"Last Wednesday."

"Jonah," she whispers so low, I almost miss it then her tears start to flow from her eyes again.

"I figured someone was trying to tell me something. I stopped fighting it. Since the day you left me standing here, I have questioned my reasons for going back. I'm thinking you were brought into my life for so many reasons, Rickie."

"What do you mean?"

"I think I was meant to fall in love with you. Watch the work you do with the wounded warriors who have to make changes in their lives because of what was taken from them while serving for their country. I'm one of the lucky ones. Sure, I have dreams every night, but I don't have the terror that some come home with and fight day after day. I don't need to be back on the front line to help my country. I can help those here at home and in the meantime, convince the woman I happen to fall in love with to spend the rest of her life with me."

"I need your phone number."

Not the response I was expecting from basically proposing. "What?"

"I have no way of getting a hold of you. We never exchanged phone numbers."

"Rickie, I'm asking you to spend the rest of your life with me."

CHAPTER THIRTEEN

Rickie

"I needed your phone number," I repeated.

Last Wednesday, he was on a plane to leave, and I was in a bathroom finding out I was going to have a baby, his baby.

He needs to know and I need to do it before I answer his question. "Tristan, I'm pregnant."

Silence! He was already looking at me like I had lost my mind when I told him I needed his phone number, now he is looking at me like I just grew a second head. My heart sinks a little lower in my chest with every second that ticks by as I wait for him to say something.

Finally, he blinks a couple of times. "When did you find out?"

"Last Wednesday."

He takes a step back and runs his hands over his face.

"I didn't have a number for you, I have been trying to get up the nerve to call your sister and ask her how to get a hold of you."

He looks like he wants to run, that's the final string of hope holding up my heart. It feels like it falls to my feet and once again tears spring from my eyes. "I'm sorry."

Those two words seem to knock him around a little, because he finally comes back and instantly I'm in his arms.

"No, I'm the one who is sorry."

"I'm not telling you this to make you stay, Tristan."

"Rickie, have you not heard a word I have said. I'm not going back, you mean more to me and I have found another way to help out my team here. Helping those who haven't been able to return, my team has a few, and then those who weren't on my team. I'm going to marry you and we are going to have a baby."

His lips cover mine before I can respond. "I can't tell you goodbye, you healed me!" his lips whisper against mine.

The End

ABOUT THE AUTHOR

Tonya Clark lives in Southern California with her hot firefighter hubby and two amazing daughters. She writes contemporary romance featuring second chance, sports, MC, shifters, suspense, and deaf culture-inspired by her youngest daughter.

When not hiding in the office writing, Tonya has the amazing job of photographing hot cover models, coaching multiple soccer teams, and running her day job.

Tonya believes everyone deserves their Happily Ever After!

Sign-up for Tonya's newsletter at www.tonyaclarkbooks.com for book news and you can find all of her books on Amazon.

- facebook.com/authortonyaclark
- twitter.com/AuthortonyaC
- instagram.com/authortonyaclark
- goodreads.com/authortonyaclark
- bookbub.com/authors/tonya-clark
- amazon.com/author/tonyaclark

ALSO BY TONYA CLARK

Sign of Love Series

Silent Burn

Silent Distraction

Silent Protection

Silent Forgiveness

Sign of Love Circle

Shift

Standalone

Retake

Driven Roads

Entangled Rivals (Book 3 Raven Boys Series) Multiple Author Series

Anthologies

Storybook Pub

Storybook Pub Christmas Wishes

Storybook Pub 2

Young Crush

Made in the USA
Monee, IL
10 July 2022